Someday

Is Not a Day of the Week

Denise Brennan-Nelson

Illustrated by Kevin O'Malley

Sleeping Bear Press

310 North Main Street, Suite 300
Chelsea, MI 48118
www.sleepingbearpress.com

THOMSON
GALE

© 2005 Thomson Gale, a part of the Thomson Corporation.

Thomson, Star Logo and Sleeping Bear Press are trademarks
and Gale is a registered trademark used herein under license.

Printed and bound in Canada.

10 9 8 7 6 5 4 3 2 1

Library of Congress Cataloging-in-Publication Data

Brennan-Nelson, Denise.
Someday is not a day of the week / written by Denise Brennan-Nelson ;
illustrated by Kevin O'Malley.
p. cm.
Summary: When asking to go on various outings, Max always
receives the answer "Someday" from adults, but with a little help from
the days of the week, he discovers where "Someday" lives.
ISBN 1-58536-243-3
[1. Days—Fiction. 2. Parent and child—Fiction.] I. O'Malley, Kevin, 1961- ill. II.
Title.

PZ7.B75165So 2005
[E]—dc22   2004027297

To Dad, whose passion for living inspired this story.
This is living!

—Big D

Max and Momma sat at the kitchen table together.
Max ate blueberry waffles while Momma made a list of the things
she had to do that day. It looked very long and boring to Max.

He smiled, thinking of all the things he would like to put on Momma's list.

"Let's go to the fair today!" he said through a mouthful of waffles.

Momma had a lot to think about so she didn't answer him right away.
Finally, without looking up, Momma softly sighed and said,
"Someday, Max, but not today."

Max slowly wrote his name in the warm, gooey syrup
while Momma added more things to her list.

When the telephone rang, Max got to it first.
Snatching it up, he asked, "Who's calling, please?"

"Hi, Max, it's Grandpa!"

"Hi, Grandpa. When are you coming to see me?
Please come today!" Max pleaded. "The fish are biting!"

Grandpa's chuckle made Max smile. "I wish I could but
Grandma and I have some errands we need to do.
We'll go fishing someday, Max, but not today."

Errands didn't sound as much fun as fishing to Max, but he didn't say that.

He wanted to tell Grandpa about his missing tooth, his enormous pet frog,
and his baseball trophy, but Momma's hand was outstretched, waiting.

"I'll have the fishing poles ready for us, Grandpa,"
Max said before handing Momma the sticky phone.

Daddy came into the kitchen and bent down to give Max a kiss.

Max flung his arms around Daddy's neck. Squeezing tightly, he whispered,
"I wish you didn't have to go to work today."

"Me too, Champ," Daddy said. "But I have a busy schedule.
I promise, we'll take a day and do something really special, just you and me."

Max's eyes grew big and hopeful. "Could you build me a fort?"

Daddy smiled and said, "Sure, Max."

"When, Daddy?" Max needed to know. "WHEN?"

Glancing at his watch, Daddy stood up and said,
"Someday, Max, but not today."

With a big sigh, Max hopped down from his chair.
He took the calendar off the wall and headed for his room.
Flopping down on his bed, Max began to sing the
song he had learned in preschool:

"Sunday, Monday, Tuesday, Wednesday, Thursday, Friday, Saturday...
Now we start again."

But wait, something wasn't right.

Slower this time and pointing at the days on the calendar, Max began again:
"Sun-day, Mon-day, Tues-day, Wednes-day, Thurs-day, Fri-day, Sa-tur-day..."

Max was confused. "Where IS Someday?" he asked out loud.

"Someday is NOT a day of the week!" a chorus of tiny voices replied.

Max's eyes darted around the room, then back to the calendar.
"What did you say?" he asked.

"Someday is NOT a day of the week!"
the voices repeated a little louder.

Bewildered, Max asked, "Who are you?"

"We're the days of the week!"

"What are you doing here?" Max asked.

Monday leaned forward and said, "We're here to help you, Max.
We heard you were looking for Someday!"

"Do you know where Someday is?" Max asked.

"No one knows for sure and that's the problem," Saturday said.

"But he'll be really busy if he ever shows up!" Wednesday blurted out.

"Why ARE you looking for Someday?" Tuesday asked.

"I have some very important things to do," Max said.
"Everyone tells me we have to wait for Someday. I have to find him!"

"Don't waste time waiting for Someday, Max," **Friday** said.

"Friday's right," **Thursday** added.
"Someday is NOT a day of the week. But you have us. We're always here."

"But you don't have any room!" Max said.

"We can always make room for the things that matter most," **Sunday** said kindly.
"If you want to do something, Max, don't wait for Someday, pick one of us."

"Momma! Momma!" Max shouted, "We can't go to the fair someday!"

"Why not?" Momma asked.

"Because someday is not a day of the week!
We have to pick one of these!" Max exclaimed, waving the calendar.

Momma sat down next to Max. Hugging him tenderly, she said, "You're right, Max, I never thought of it like that! What day should we go?"

Max didn't hesitate. "How 'bout Tuesday?"

Momma thought for a moment, and then shaking her head she said, "We can't go on Tuesday, Max, I have to..."

Max swallowed hard. She doesn't understand, he thought. Sadly, he walked back to his bedroom.

Momma looked at the piles of laundry and thought about her long to-do list.

Then she thought about what Max had said.

Poking her head into Max's room, Momma said, "I found someday!"

"Really?" Max asked. "Where?"

"Get your shoes, Max…"

And to his delight, on Saturday Max and Daddy ate lunch
in the most unbelievable blanket fort Max had ever seen.

And on the following Sunday,
after showing Grandpa his missing tooth,
his enormous pet frog,
and his baseball trophy…

Max and Grandpa went fishing.